MONSTER SQUAD
THEY CAME FROM PLANET Q

BY LAURA DOWER
ILLUSTRATED BY DAVE SCHLAFMAN

GROSSET & DUNLAP
An Imprint of Penguin Group (USA) Inc.

GROSSET & DUNLAP

Published by the Penguin Group

Penguin Group (USA) Inc., 375 Hudson Street, New York, New York 10014, USA

Penguin Group (Canada), 90 Eglinton Avenue East, Suite 700, Toronto, Ontario M4P
2Y3, Canada (a division of Pearson Penguin Canada Inc.)

Penguin Books Ltd., 80 Strand, London WC2R 0RL, England

Penguin Group Ireland, 25 St. Stephen's Green, Dublin 2, Ireland
(a division of Penguin Books Ltd.)

Penguin Group (Australia), 250 Camberwell Road, Camberwell, Victoria 3124,
Australia (a division of Pearson Australia Group Pty. Ltd.)

Penguin Books India Pvt. Ltd., 11 Community Centre, Panchsheel Park, New
Delhi–110 017, India

Penguin Group (NZ), 67 Apollo Drive, Rosedale, North Shore 0632, New Zealand
(a division of Pearson New Zealand Ltd.)

Penguin Books (South Africa) (Pty.) Ltd., 24 Sturdee Avenue,
Rosebank, Johannesburg 2196, South Africa

Penguin Books Ltd., Registered Offices: 80 Strand, London WC2R 0RL, England

Library of Congress Control Number: 2009045218

ISBN 978-0-448-44915-9   10 9 8 7 6 5 4 3 2 1

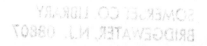

For Papa.

        —Laura Dower

To Dad.

        —Dave Schlafman

Acknowledgments:
Special thanks to Dave
Schlafman's magic pen.
Extra special thanks to
Judy Goldschmidt and
she knows why.

TABLE OF CONTENTS

PROLOGUE

LINDSEY GOMEZ

I ripped off silver birthday wrapping paper, lifted a pale pink box lid, and tore through a bunch of sparkly tissue.

There it was.

"A CAMERA? NO WAY!" I cried.

"What do you mean *no way*?" Dad joked. "All we ever give you are cameras."

"Yeah, I know," I said, smirking. "This makes camera number twenty-two in my collection!"

Kids at school know me as "photographer at large" because I snap photos for the school paper. I try to show up at all soccer games, school musicals, and spelling bees. And now that I'm a member of the Monster Squad, photography comes in handy more than ever. I'm working on a photo scrapbook of all our Monster Squad adventures.

Monster Squad is this top secret group formed by genius B-Monster movie director Oswald Leery. A few months back, Leery and his sidekick, Walter Block, invited four of us Riddle Elementary fifth-graders (and superfans of the B-Monster movies) to join him and track down B-Monsters in the real world.

How do B-Monsters get out into the world, you ask? Well, when a Leery B-Monster movie is screened from an original movie reel, the B-Monster has the ability to escape. If you were stuck in a movie reel, wouldn't you want out?

When Leery explained this all to me, I jumped right on the bandwagon because . . . well, I couldn't think of a single reason not to. I could not turn away the chance to hunt down B-Monsters *and* take photos at the same time! After all, my grandpa Max was the original photographer and cinematographer for all of Leery's movies.

And I inherited his photography gene—big time.

An entire wall of my bedroom is covered with cool B-Monster photos that my grandpa took on and off the movie set. He has shots of B-Monsters attacking, eating, and flying warp speed into the ozone layer.

My favorite shot shows a bunch of glowing robot props from *They Came from Planet Q*—with Grandpa posing in the middle.

I inherited more than a photo gene from Grandpa though; I inherited most of his camera collection, too. Many of the cameras are old-fashioned, like the ones that take sepia-toned pictures (brown and white instead of black-and-white), but they work like new. There are Polaroid-type cameras (where the picture comes right out); cameras with long-range lenses; and cameras that have a special "B-Monster Vision" knob.

"Was this really one of Grandpa's cameras?" I asked my parents. "It looks so plain."

"Came from his secret stash, I guess," Mom explained. "It was at the bottom of a box in the attic, all wrapped up in brown paper with a bunch of other movie props. At first we thought it was broken. The lens was scratched a bit and that dial on top was covered with grime. But then your father found this new repair shop . . ."

"Reely Good Things!" Dad piped up. "It's a brand-new store at Petroglyph Mall down on the lower level. They sell cameras and DVDs. I saw some B-Monster movies in the shop. I wouldn't be surprised if they have some original reels there!"

"Original reels?" I gulped.

I knew what that meant. A new B-Monster could be released at any moment. The squad already eliminated three. I wasn't really sure I was ready for number four.

My dad knows Petroglyph Mall like the back of his hand. He's the head of security there. Twenty-six different guys report to him! He knows all the store owners, which is a major bonus, because they offer cool discounts and specials, like offering to fix my new camera.

"Thanks for this," I said, squeezing my arms around both Mom and Dad at the same time. "You get the best presents."

"Well . . ." Mom shrugged. "You're the best daughter."

Dad nodded at the camera. "Looks pretty interesting . . ."

"More like pretty *strange*," I said. "What are all these functions?"

There were tiny icons on the dial on top: an amoeba, a bird, a sun, a moon, a candle, a question mark, and even a lightning bolt coming out of a cloud—only the bolt was red.

"Lightning bolts usually mean some kind of flash," I said, in answer to my own question. "But I've never seen red lightning."

I aimed the lens at my parents. No sooner had I snapped than the camera sizzled like a BBQ.

"Just say cheesy!" I called out.

My parents were such big show-offs. They couldn't stop posing. Dad crossed his arms in front of him like a rap singer. Mom fluffed up her hair and smiled like she was in a pageant.

After a few minutes, however, Dad shouted, "Okay! Enough of this. Time to move on to part two!"

My jaw dropped. "What do you mean, part *two*?"

"Part two of your present, of course," Dad said.

Mom nudged me toward the basement stairs. "No peeking!" she said.

Had they finally—finally!—gotten me the puppy I'd been begging for since I was three? No. Wait. It couldn't possibly be a pup. Mom was allergic. Was it games? Books? *Another* camera with even more dials?

"Open your eyes," Dad finally said.

I just barely opened one eye first; then the second.

The room was dark, so it took a minute for me to adjust. But then I saw everything.

Everything.

It nearly knocked me flat.

"A DARKROOM? Aaaaaaaaaaaaaaah!" I wailed. "Someone pinch me. Is this really happening? I can't believe it—no way!"

Mom and Dad looked very, *very* pleased with themselves.

"So what do you think?" Mom asked. "Happy?"

"Happy? I need a tissue I'm so happy!" I blubbered. "Now I can develop all my photos on my own! Thank you! Thank you!"

"Thank Grandpa Max," Dad said. "Before he passed away, he made us promise that you would get this darkroom. It just took me some time to fix it up right. Now it's yours. Mom and I think you have the potential to be a great photographer, Lindsey."

The darkroom had always been in the basement, but it hadn't been used in years. Dad fixed it up with tubs and trays, photographic chemicals, a sink, and shelves of boxes (mostly filled with photo paper). My parents installed a photo drying line, a new timer, and special darkroom lights, too.

"Is this really all for me?" I asked.

My parents nodded.

"Well!" Mom cheered. "Shall we go back upstairs and celebrate with some birthday cake? I made carrot with cream cheese frosting just the way you like it."

When we got upstairs, Mom and Dad sang "Happy Birthday to Our Wonderful Daughter!" as Mom sliced the enormous cake slabs for each of us. Then Dad clicked on the television, just like usual. At six o'clock every night, we watch *Word Buzz* on channel five. We smacked the table edge like it was an imaginary word buzzer and pretended that we were actual contestants on the show.

I wasn't really watching TV so much because I was looking at my camera. But just as the game show host shouted out a super-duper-double bonus question, I glanced up—right in time to see the TV screen go black.

An announcer's voice barked. "We interrupt this regularly scheduled program for an eeeeeemergency news bulletin . . ."

Talking heads filled the screen. Dad turned up the volume.

"Chaos across the globe!" cried a newscaster.

Along the bottom of the TV screen, words flashed in lime green:

UFO SIGHTED IN BOLIVIAN JUNGLE . . .
STRANGE ENERGY FORCE REPORTED
IN THE RED SEA . . .
SCREECHING ANIMALS FLEE
SWEDISH ZOO AS STEEL CAGES
COLLAPSE . . .

Dad flipped channels. But the channels were all the same, with warnings galore. Even WNN, the Weather News Network, was raising a red flag. Dad flipped to WNN and saw a spinning cyclone and the words: TSUNAMI DOOM!

"Tsunami *doom*?" Dad cried. "Hmmmmph. What's *really* going on?"

"Global warming, I'll bet," Mom grumbled. "If it's not a melting ice cap, it's pollution in the sky . . . and now *this*."

She grabbed the remote and clicked the television off.

"Wait! Mom!" I wailed. "We were watching that!"

"Not anymore," Mom said sweetly. "This is your special birthday night. No bad news or hot topics allowed. How about another slice of cake?"

I sighed. "Moooom." But it did no good. I took the slice.

Of course, at that moment, I probably should have known what was *really* going on out there in the world. I should have clicked the TV right back on and taken pages of notes. After all, as a member of the Monster Squad, it's my job to pay extra-close attention to freaky occurrences just like those.

Often, it's a sign of B-Force.

B-Force is the incredible power generated by the presence of a real, live B-Monster. B-Force may take the form of wild weather or a bug swarm or even a river of goo. No matter what form it takes, B-Force always means the same thing: Some B-Monster is coming to town.

Rrrrrrrrrrrrrring.

Mom handed the phone right to me. "Who's Stella?" she asked.

There was only one Stella that I knew in the whole world and she was in the Monster Squad like me. Other kids in Riddle call her Ninja because she's got a mean karate kick.

"Lindsey?" Stella's voice crackled. "You watching TV? You sitting down? Because right now channels 6,

8, *and* 10 are showing this extreme stuff happening all over the planet. And you know what *that* usually means . . ."

"I know," I whispered. "B-Force . . ."

I didn't want Mom or Dad to hear. Neither is allowed to know the inner workings of the Monster Squad or the truth about all the real-life B-Monsters that have been on the loose. Mom would have a cow if she knew I was moonlighting as Lindsey the B-Hunter.

"So we need to meet!" Stella said. "It's too late to meet tonight so let's hook up at the mall tomorrow. Food court. Eleven AM. I'll call Jesse. You call Damon. Got it?"

I got it. I dialed Damon right away. An answering machine picked up and I explained the plan.

"B-there, or B-square!" I blurted into the receiver at the end.

A massive B-Monster takeover may have been brewing, but that wasn't about to stop little old me from making a pun.

CHAPTER 1

READ 'EM
AND WEEP

When we're not meeting at school or Leery Castle, Monster Squad meets at Petroglyph Mall. Sometimes Dad even arranges for us to get food court discounts. Lunch that day was served at Wok N Roll. Nothing like planning B-Monster destruction with a side order of rice.

The mall is called Petroglyph because it's supposedly built on top of these old, haunted, cavemen-painted caves. A petroglyph is a caveman's cave picture, complete with stick figures and bows and arrows. All the rumors about the mall being haunted don't scare me, but they do set a good mood for plotting and planning.

Jesse, as usual, came prepared for a meeting. Super-prepared.

He threw a stack of important papers onto the table.

"Read 'em and weep, Monster Squad," Jesse said. "Evidence of B-Force all over the world! This is one bad B-Monster."

He'd been up late last night, printing out dozens of stories he'd found on the Internet. They were stranger-than-strange-but-true stories that pointed to some kind of powerful B-Monster presence.

"Check out *that* headline!" Damon said, pointing to one of the stories.

MICROWAVE OVENS DISAPPEAR INTO THIN AIR

"*Nuke* kidding," I cackled. "Who *cooked* up that disaster?"

"Awwwww, Lindsey," Jesse said, laughing. "That's just lame . . ."

"And lamer," Damon added.

I made a sourball face and read the piece aloud, anyway.

RAMBO, IN—Officials in Rambo were stunned when the Kitchenette Factory, which produces supplies and appliances, came under an apparent attack. Yesterday morning at approximately seven AM, the roof to the company building appeared to open up like a volcano. Passersby reported seeing a large cloud of red, hazy smoke. Refrigerators, ovens, dishwashers, garbage compactors, and microwaves seemed to lift up into the air through the gap in the roof and disappear into the smoke. Kitchenette president, Herb Splutter, said, "We suspect foul play." Company representatives are working with law enforcement to investigate the bizarre incident.

"Foul play?" I joked again. "What? Like a bunch of chickens stole all the microwave ovens?"

No laughs. Just groans. *Loud* groans.

"What do these stories mean?" Stella said, flipping through the pages Jesse had brought.

"Hey, read this one!" Damon cried, pointing to yet another article.

BARCELONA (INTERNATIONAL)—Esteemed Museo Magnifico curator Rolando Miguel de Cervantes is recovering in the hospital tonight following the strange events that took place inside the city museum last night. Numerous antiquities and an entire collection of knightly armor disappeared in the middle of the night. Mr. de Cervantes was knocked out by a steel sword as it left the building. There is no evidence to indicate who took the sword or the rest of the museum inventory. No other people were seen at the scene. Police are checking security cameras at the scene as well as the alarm system. Museo Magnifico is closed until further notice.

"Museo Magnifico isn't the only heist," Jesse said, glancing at the pages. "There are articles here about armor and jewelry stolen from other places, too."

We looked at the other articles about places whose names I could hardly spell, like Czechoslovakia and Zimbabwe. There was a town in Australia where every single lawnmower vanished into thin air.

What B-Monster could be that powerful? There were so many possibilities.

"Okay. Armor, lawnmowers, appliances . . ." Jesse started to list off the subjects in all the articles.

"Wait!" Stella blurted. "Everything you just mentioned is made of the same thing: metal."

I gave Stella a high five. "Impressive observation, Ninja," I said.

"Actually, if you want to be accurate, they're all made from alloys of metal," Jesse added.

"Huh?" Damon said, looking befuddled.

"In alloys, the metal is not pure but rather a combination of numerous different metals that make up the many varying levels of—"

"WHOA!" Damon yelped. "Stop, please! We get it, bro. What *don't* you know?"

"Well," Jesse said, "I don't know what B-Monster we're dealing with. Do you?"

"This can't be too hard to figure out," I said. "If the B-Force involves metal objects . . . then what does that say about our B-Monster?"

"That maybe it's magnetic?" Jesse observed.

"Whoa," Damon shook his head. "You know what? There are a lot of magnetic B-Monsters."

"Excellent!" I said. "So let's start there . . ."

Brrrrrrrrrraaaaaaaw! Brrrrrrrraaoooooo!

All at once, a mall alarm went off. It sounded like a dying Brontosaurus. We covered our ears.

"What *is* that?" Damon asked.

"It's coming from the lower level of the mall," I said. "Let's go look."

We left Wok N' Roll, passed a dozen more food court stalls, and leaned over the railing to see what was going on down below.

And there it was—unbelievable!

Just outside the Toy Mania boutique was the strangest parade of toys. Playstations, Xboxes, remote controls, battery packs, race cars, handheld radios, and a whole slew of other junk had come to life and started walking in formation. Leading the way was a toy monkey with little, crashing cymbals and motorized wheels.

And everything in the parade was *metal*. Maybe they were being pulled by a magnetic force?

"Follow that monkey parade!" Damon cried.

This was getting *so* weird. And we weren't the only ones sensing B-Force. I could hear people downstairs freaking out a little, too.

"This mall is cursed!"

"Nah, haunted!"

"Run away!"

One woman in the crowd actually yelled, "It's the end of the world!"

"Let's go down and get a closer look," Jesse said, nudging me. "Maybe the parade will lead us to the B-Monster."

We made a fast break for the escalator.

SOMEONE FLICKED A CRAZY SWITCH!

Naturally, the escalator was jammed with people. Everyone wanted out of the mall at the exact same time.

I raised my new camera up over my head and began clicking random photos of the puzzled crowd. But as I snapped pictures, the camera snapped a fuse or something. It let out this blinding white flash and made a sizzle sound. Then it glowed hot. I nearly dropped it on the escalator step.

Damon saw it glow, too. "Oooh," he blurted. "That looks a lot like one of Leery's cameras . . ."

"Really?" I asked. I couldn't remember ever seeing this before. "From where?"

"One of the movies . . ."

"Which one?"

But Damon couldn't remember which one.

Even a B-Encyclopedia gets brain freeze once in a while. He pulled a crumpled list of Bs from his back pocket and scanned the movie titles. In the world of Leery's Bs, there were so many monsters it was hard to keep track of them. We sometimes used this list to help ID our B-Monsters.

"Look for movies with a magnetic B-Monster and a camera," I said.

"Okay." Damon read the names: "There's Robototron. That B-Monster was metal. He's a possibility."

"I don't recall a camera in *Robototron*," Jesse said.

"All right, well . . . there are other Bs on this list that fit our profile, too," Damon said, scanning the paper.

"What about *Iron Dino*?" Stella asked.

"Not that B," Damon frowned. "Iron Dino was just a fake, prehistoric B-Monster that *looked* like he was made of metal. Not magnetic at all."

"What about Dr. Disaster?" I asked. "He worked in a steel-encased lab. That *had* to be magnetic."

"Didn't he have arms of steel, too?" Stella asked, high-fiving me.

"Well, c*laws* of steel," Damon said, shaking

his head. "But Dr. Disaster was only three feet tall, remember? He operated from inside a mechanical cow."

"Yeah," Stella said, "but the cow was metal, too, right?"

"Stella . . ." Damon said. "It wasn't Dr. D."

"Oh, sure," Stella said. "Just shoot down my answer just because—"

"Guys." I tapped my foot nervously. The whole mall was falling apart and Stella and Damon wanted to pick a fight with each other?

Typical.

"Hey, what about the robots from *They Came from Planet Q*?" Damon said, "Remember them? They were held together by magnetic force! When they came to Earth, they nearly destroyed the planet."

"Yeah," I said. "They were powered by that crazy, red rock . . ."

"Firequartz!" Jesse exclaimed. "It magnetized the robots!"

The escalator arrived at the lower level and the four of us jumped off. It was hard not to get body-slammed, but we dove into the mob, anyway.

People were really talking now. Apparently,

the credit card machines were all still down. Jesse pointed out that credit cards can be erased by high levels of magnetism.

Hmmmmmm.

Up ahead of us, the metal toy parade continued, cymbals clanging. We followed it.

"Leery says there's safety in numbers," Stella reminded us. "So we must stick together, no matter what."

We moved through the sea of frenzied people as quickly as possible, eyes fixed on the parade as best we could. After a few yards, when the toys switched direction, we did, too. I jumped onto a bench to see where the toys were headed. The others jumped onto the bench with me.

"Look!" I cried, pointing. "The toys are headed toward the center of the mall. Why are they going to the center of the mall? What's there?"

"Something magnetic?" Stella asked.

"Our B-Monster?" Jesse said.

I snapped a photo and turned to Damon to find out what he thought.

But he wasn't there.

"Damon?"

I spun back around the other way.

"DAMON?"

I craned my neck to see where he'd gone and nearly tripped over a kid in the process. My camera fell to the floor and the flash went off. *Snap! Snap! Snap!*

"DAMOOOOOOON!"

"Anyone see where Damon went?" Jesse asked.

"Green shirt! Twelve o'clock!" Stella howled, pointing over the heads of the crowd.

Lucky for us, Damon's neon "Tuff Guy" T-shirt made him easy to spot, even among all this chaos.

We raced over and caught up to him in no time.

"What are you doing, Damon?" Stella howled.

"We do things together. We're Monster Squad; not Chicken Squad."

"I'm not a chicken," Damon said. "I was just getting a head start . . ."

"Nice lie," Stella huffed and assumed her Ninja pose. "I mean, nice *try*."

"Hey!" I yelled. "The toys are flying!"

All those metal toys suddenly became airborne as if they were attached to some kind of invisible bungee cord. It was amazing to watch.

Up, up, up . . .

CRAAAAASSSSH!

We stopped dead in our tracks. I grabbed Jesse's arm so hard I probably twisted off all the freckles.

Directly above us, the ceiling had ripped open. There was a gaping hole the size of a football field.

"Wow," I said. "It's not every day that the ceiling of our local mall opens wide and says *ahhhhh*."

"I've never seen anything like this on the *Science Man* show," Jesse said. He tried to look up into the hole, but there was dust and debris floating around in the air. It made it hard to see anything.

"It's like there's a giant magnet in the sky pulling all the metal objects its way," Damon noted.

We all squinted and tried to see what might be hanging over the mall ceiling.

And then, just like that, we felt a spray of water rain down on our heads.

"What in the middle of Riddle was THAT?" I gulped.

THREE ^THOUSAND^ COINS IN A FOUNTAIN

The center of the mall is all about the enormous Petroglyph fountain. People sit on the ledge to take a break from shopping. They toss in coins for luck. They make wishes.

But at that very moment, that fountain was going bonkers. All the coins were spouting through the air!

"This is just like those lawnmowers in Australia!" I said.

All around us, the mall fountain gushed and sprayed. For a split second, I wondered if all those coins spewing into the air might just come crashing back down onto our heads. Talk about pennies from heaven!

"So now that we know there is some magnetic B-Force up there, with the power to suck up all the toys and steel beams and coins from inside the mall, what can we do about it?" asked Stella.

My body shook. I didn't know anything right now except that the water was cold and I was a bundle of nerves. Watching all these metal objects get sucked into the sky really did make me wonder if the world was going to end. I could only imagine how scary all this B-Force (even just a little of it) must have looked to a non-Monster Squadder.

"Should we get out of here like everyone else?" Jesse asked cautiously. I sensed a little fear in his voice.

I knew Damon was ready to run. I was literally holding him back. I hooked my arms through his.

But it was all for nothing. Because leaving now was definitely *not* an option.

"I think we should go up and investigate," I said. "There are all sorts of secret passages and places inside this mall. If there's a big magnet out there, it must have left some clues on the roof, right?"

"That hole is waaaaaay up high," Damon said. "How do we get all the way up there?"

"Well," Jesse said thoughtfully. "We could all get dressed in metal suits and then the giant magnet will pull *us* up . . ."

"JESSE!" Stella yelped. "Would you get serious?"

"Look, there are all sorts of secret passages in the mall," I said. "My dad has maps of the entire mall complex in his office. We could check out the maps and see what's marked on the different levels. Maybe we'll be able to locate our B-Monster that way."

As we stood there, the Toy Mania alarm finally stopped ringing and the fountain stopped running water. Everything stopped, actually . . . except the pounding of my chest.

And then, like a cannon, a voice boomed behind me and I nearly fell over onto the ground.

"Lindsey Monica Gomez! What are YOU doing here?!"

TREMORS!

I turned and saw Dad. I could tell he was mad because his neck was cherry Popsicle red.

"Answer me. What are you doing here?"

"Dad!" I said. "We were up at the food court when we heard noises and we—"

"G-g-got scared," Damon interrupted.

"Correction. *You* got scared, Damon," Stella said.

"Scared?" Dad said, tugging on his shirt collar. "Well, I should say so! The entire mall is being evacuated. My guys are rounding up people in the mall. The fire and rescue team is coming in. Just look at this place! This is dangerous and intense . . ."

Dad's walkie-talkie crackled.

"Whoa," Damon said. "Your *dad* is the one that's intense."

"Lindsey, I need you and your crew to vamoose . . .

NOW!" Dad barked, checking his walkie-talkie again. "Evacuation orders mean *everyone*, young lady, even the daughter of the head of security."

Dad asked Big Wally, the biggest security guard on the team, to escort us all the way out of the mall.

"Great," Stella whispered to me as we moved toward the door. "We are just about to ID the B-Monster—and this happens."

"Wait! Dad!" I said, turning back. "I know we're just kids, Dad, but I think you should know there's something else going on . . . something magnetic is . . ."

"LINDSEY!"

The boys glared. I knew I shouldn't have hinted at our mission, but I had to say something! We couldn't just leave! We couldn't just let ourselves be escorted from the scene of the B-Monster!

"Go home, Lindsey," Dad said sternly. Big Wally took me and the others by the arms.

I wanted to tug myself loose and run back to make one final plea to Dad, but just then the building shuddered.

Lights flickered.

And the whole place went dark with a loud *hissssssssss.*

"POWER! OUT!" someone yelled. I heard Dad yell, too. We were in a cave with voices shouting out in the darkness.

Damon found me first. "W-w-what's going on?" he squealed, clinging to my side like a vine. "Is this it? Is this the end of the world?"

"WHERE IS EVERYONE?" Stella yelped. She was close by, but where?

"I'm over here," Big Wally boomed.

"Me too," Stella said.

"Did the floor just move?" Jesse cried. "Because I felt the floor move."

"Oh noooooooo!" Damon wailed. I think he wanted to run away, but he couldn't even see a foot in front of him.

Once again, the building shimmied and shook.

"Lindsey!"

I heard Dad's voice and then he was next to me. Just like that. Somehow, in the muddle of the darkness, he found me.

"Lindsey, honey, are you okay?" Dad whispered softly. He's just as good at being sweet as he is at being firm. "Look, I want you to stay calm. There have been these faint tremors all week at the mall and just a little while ago, security reported a crack in the atrium ceiling, but we have a backup . . ."

Brrrrrrrrrrmmmmmmmmmm.

Just like that, a motor surged and hummed and the overhead mall lights buzzed on. I could see again! What a relief! I never thought I would be glad to see Damon Molloy's ugly face, but at that moment, few things could have made me happier.

I glanced around. Most ordinary people in the mall had left or been escorted out. The place was crawling with security.

"Is everyone okay?" Dad said. "I knew the backup power would kick on so we could see."

"Speaking of backing up . . . er . . ." Damon said. "*I'd* like to back up all the way to the mall exit."

"But we can't go!" I said. "We haven't found the—"

I pressed my hand over my own mouth.

Dad gave me this quizzical look. "Lindsey, is there something you're not telling me?" he asked. "You and your friends are acting awfully . . ."

"No, no, no," Stella said. "We're fine. And we'll go. We'll go right now, Mr. Gomez. Let's shuffle, Big Wally!"

None of us wanted to leave (well, except for Damon),

but there was nothing any of us could say that would change my father's mind. And before we knew it, Big Wally was leading us through the mall. And there was no arguing with Big Wally.

By the time we got to the parking lot, the crowd was going crazy. People were pushing and shouting and crying—it was pretty scary.

"Stay safe, kids!" Wally called out before turning back inside.

Safe? I thought. *Yeah, sure thing, Big Wally.*

We elbowed our way through the crowd to get to the mall entrance. But there was no way back in! Dad had security guards posted at every single entrance to the building. Our Monster Squad mission had reached its first major detour.

Now what?

"What now?" Stella whined. "Everything we desperately need is in *there*!"

I glanced around and thought hard. I snapped a few photos and then smiled at my camera.

If I've learned anything from being a photographer at large it's this: A camera can sometimes see things the eye can't.

"Not *everything*."

CHAPTER 5

LET'S SEE WHAT DEVELOPS

"I guess it's time to come up with another plan," Jesse started to say.

"You mean a plan *B*?" I cracked.

"Oh, come on!" Stella cried. "This is really not a time for jokes, Lindsey!"

"Do you three want to come over to my house for a little while?" I suggested. "It's just up the street . . ."

We headed around one parking lot and into another. I'd never seen this place so busy. And then we saw something even weirder than the spouting coin fountain or the hole in the ceiling.

At least five sports cars had been stacked like blocks, one on top of the other. The pile looked ready to topple over, but it didn't. Something was keeping the cars stacked and stuck.

"Extreme magnetic force!" Jesse cried.

I snapped a few photos of the car pileup.

Then Damon noticed there was another pile of metal objects . . . and another. Toys from Toy Mania, steel beams, chairs, and anything else that was metal and not nailed down headed up into the darkening sky. As we stood there, a small yellow car was sucked from its parking space and deposited with a loud *smash* onto one of the piles.

Where was an air traffic controller when you needed one? The objects were in some kind of magnetic holding pattern right here in the parking lot.

Now I'm not an A+ science student like Jesse, but I knew this much: Whatever B-Monster was on its way had a herculean magnetic force. I felt all twitchy just watching it. If we didn't confirm this B-Monster soon and figure out a way to stop it, the entire town of Riddle would probably turn into one giant magnet.

"We ruled out Robototron and Dr. Disaster already," Stella said. "So what magnetic B-Monsters are left?"

"Did anyone mention *Escape to Skull Island*?" I asked. "Wasn't that island magnetic?"

"Not really," Jesse replied. "It was radioactive and I suppose it probably might have had increased levels of magnetism, but . . ."

"Forget *Skull Island*, brainiac!" Damon blurted. "I swear our B-Monster is from *They Came from Planet Q*. Those robots came down to Earth from the sky."

"Right!" I said, looking up.

"You are right, Damon," Jesse said. "We know the B-Force is coming from the sky. Good work."

We left the parking lot together and walked down the street to my big, old Victorian house with blue shutters. Damon filled us in with the many things he remembered about the *They Came from Planet Q* flick. The detail that intrigued me the most was that the hero in the movie carried a simple-looking camera that had secret powers.

Mom must have seen us race up the walkway. She greeted us with my usual snack, popcorn and juice, even though she didn't really know who my Monster Squad friends were.

She said she'd heard the sirens at the mall, but

had no idea what was going on there. I guess Dad didn't want Mom to freak out, so he hadn't called to tell her about the mass evacuation of the mall or the ceiling that wasn't. The whole crisis hadn't been broadcast by the news yet, either. It was hard to believe she'd been missing all the action, but she had. And I wasn't about to let on that I knew anything unusual.

Once inside the house, I told everyone to follow me quietly down to the basement.

"WOW!" Stella said once we got downstairs. "That looks like a darkroom."

"That's because it *is* a darkroom," I said, grinning at Stella.

Everyone glanced at my camera.

"Right! Let's develop the photographs you took at the mall with your new camera!" Jesse said.

"My thoughts exactly," I said.

"Maybe you have a photo of the B-Monster in there!" Stella said.

"My thoughts exactly," I said again, grinning.

I hoped this camera had somehow captured some image that would confirm the identity of our latest B-Monster.

The other Monster Squadders helped me pull down the trays for the different developing chemicals.

"Let's see what develops," I said, as we got to work setting it up.

Once the safety light was on, I removed the film from my camera and cut the negatives. Then I transferred those images onto photo paper. Gently, I dipped each sheet of photo paper into one tub with chemicals, and then the next one, and finally rinsed off a fully developed photo and hung it on the line. I repeated the process for all the shots. Stella, Jesse, and Damon helped.

Each time a photo image began to sharpen in the final developing tub, I felt butterflies of anticipation. We all did.

"Look! It's the fountain!" Jesse cried.

And then, "Too bad it's blurred!"

I had taken so many shots. Most of the fountain photos came out fuzzy because of the moving water. Most photos of the parade from Toy Mania came out blurred, too.

But there was one amazing—and revealing—shot.

"Lindsey!" Jesse said, looking closely at the photo. "You got it!"

"Got what?" Stella looked very close. "Are those spots from the developing fluid?"

"I don't think so," I said, shaking my head. Then I grabbed a magnifying glass and handed it to Damon. "Let's have the B-Encyclopedia take a look and tell us what he sees."

Damon took a look. "Whoa."

I grabbed the photograph and hung it on the line.

Right there in black-and-white was the best and coolest proof we could have ever hoped to find.

We had an actual photograph of B-Force and our B-Monster in action.

CHAPTER 6

NO IFS, ANDS, OR BOTS

"Robots!" Damon cried. "They're all right there! The robots from *They Came from Planet Q*! I told you! I told you!"

"Lindsey, your camera saw the robots before we did? How did it do that?" asked Stella.

I shrugged. "Lucky guess?"

The truth is, when you're a Monster Squadder, incredible

things could happen at any moment. So even though I was completely flabbergasted by the B-Monsters in the photo, at the same time, I wasn't so flabbergasted, if you know what I mean.

I knew Stella was annoyed because Damon had been right about the movie and Stella likes to be the one who gets things right. But nothing mattered now—except for this photograph.

We had *finally* IDed our B-Monster.

In the photo, a cluster of the Planet Q robots were right there, leading the toy parade in the mall. Even though they had been invisible to our human eyes at the scene, Grandpa Max's camera was able to capture them on film. Clearly those robots were after something in Petroglyph Mall.

"Great work, Monster Squad," Jesse said. "There are sixty-three B-Monster flicks—some with more than one monster in them. It's hard to keep track of everything in the world of Oswald Leery . . ."

"But we keep doing it," I said.

"Damon, can you tell us more about *They Came from Planet Q*?" Jesse asked. "What else do we need to know? You're the expert on this stuff."

"Well," Damon explained. He puffed up his chest

proudly. "In *They Came from Planet Q*, there were these UFOs that circled the planet. They shape-shifted like Transformers before Transformers even existed! Even though they looked like they were held together with barely screwed in bolts, these massive, magnetic robots nearly destroyed everything on our planet . . ."

"What finally destroyed them?" Jesse asked.

Damon cleared his throat and smiled. "Roger Rogers, of course."

Roger Rogers was one of Oswald Leery's coolest superheroes. He beat a lot of B-Monsters.

I held up the photograph. "What are these glowing red bulbs on their bodies? They look like ordinary lightbulbs."

"Don't forget in the world of Oswald Leery, looks can be deceiving," Damon said. "Don't judge a B-Monster by its bolts or its bulbs."

"If Roger Rogers saves the day," I cried, "we can save the day the exact same way, right?"

"I sure hope so," Jesse said.

"This is rough," Damon said. "Bots are so much worse than slime. Worse than multiplying mantids. This is an entire *army* of angry, magnetized aliens.

In case you hadn't noticed, there are only four of us. I think this might be mission impossible."

"Look," I said. "Nothing is impossible, Damon. In previous battles against B-Monsters, there is always some trick or weakness or way to destroy the monster. It has to be the same with this. We'll find that weakness."

"Yeah, after almost every single person on the planet dies . . ." Damon sighed.

"Damon!" Stella yelled. "For someone who has so much useful information, you can be so USELESS."

"Stella," Jesse groaned. "Look, we know our B-Monster is magnetic but I think we should all go up to Leery Castle and watch the movie together again to find out *more* stuff about the B. While we're there, we can talk to Walter about a plan of action. The survival of planet Earth depends on us."

"Yes!" I cheered. "We vaporized slime! We smashed giant mantids! We faced off with a bunch of eyeballs! We can do anything!"

"Come on," Stella snarled. She assumed the ninja pose. "Let's just kick some monster butt. Lets find the bots, dunk 'em in the ocean, and rust all their bolts . . ."

"Ha!" Damon laughed. "Not bad, Stella. That would have been a great alternate ending for the original flick."

Stella cracked a smile. "You think?"

"No ifs, ands, or bots about it," I said.

CHAPTER 7

ROGER TO
THE RESCUE!

I called Walter from the phone in my room. He picked us up from my house and delivered us to Nerve Mountain in no time. That guy drives fast.

"What's that buzzing noise?" Stella asked as we entered Leery Castle.

"Aw, the dratted alarm system," Walter said. "It has been buzzing all day long. We're having a power problem. Leery Castle has gone completely kerplooey!"

"You can say that again," I said. "There are problems like that popping up all over Riddle, especially at Petroglyph Mall. This town's shutting down. Something magnetic is interfering with all the power . . ."

I told Walter about all the crazy things we had

seen at the fountain and in the parking lots. Then we showed him the robot photo.

"Definitely from *They Came from Planet Q*," Walter said. "Good work. But how did you ever catch them in a photograph like this? They have not even shown themselves in Riddle yet!"

I held up camera twenty-two. Walter's face drooped.

"That's the camera from the *They Came from Planet Q* set!" Walter cried. "It's been missing for decades. Where in the four corners of the galaxy did you get *that*?"

"Um . . . my grandpa Max," I said. "Mom and Dad gave it to me yesterday as a birthday gift."

"Ah! Max! Of course!" Walter smiled. He seemed relieved. "This was a prized prop from the movie *They Came from Planet Q*—and other movies before that. Dr. Leery thought this camera was stolen or lost years ago. I'm so happy to see it again! And that definitely explains how you got the shot of the bots."

"Nice rhyme, Walt," Damon joked.

"It was just hidden in a box in a closet," I admitted. "I guess Grandpa put it there for safekeeping."

"Well," Walter said. "You should know that

most of the knobs and buttons on the camera are meaningless. Except for one; and you've already found it. The red lightning bolt button enables the camera to pick up B-Monsters even before they're visible to your Squadder eyes."

"We know that now," I said. We all grinned.

"Well, Monster Squad," Walter said. "You've gotten very good at your job, haven't you?"

"But it doesn't really make sense," Jesse said. "Scientifically speaking, can you really take a photo of something that can't be seen?"

"Oh, Jesse!" I cried. "Use your imagination. In the world of the B-Monster, anything can happen. Haven't you learned that yet? The way to fight B-Monsters is to use a little science and a lot of imagination."

Weeee-oooo. Weeeee-ooooo.

All at once, the castle alarms went off even louder than before. We covered our ears.

"I have to go check the castle's communication system," Walter told us. "We're trying to get it back online. You can call Leery yourself and tell him what you've discovered. He will be thrilled."

Walter handed us an enormous bag of larva crunch, our favorite, cheesy castle snack.

"Take this," Walter said as he left the room to go and turn the alarms off. "Get the copy of *They Came from Planet Q* from the vault. I'll meet you in the screening room. Hopefully you can watch it before the power short-circuits again."

My head whirred like a pinwheel.

I had so many questions, but there was so little time for answers. We needed the movie screening. We needed a Leery pep talk. Even though we'd made some smart guesses so far today, this B-Monster still intimidated me.

We found our DVD copy of *They Came from Planet Q* and headed for the screening room. Getting into the screening room might very well be my favorite part of being on the Monster Squad. We get to go down a slide that lands us in our individual, cushy, floating theater seats.

Although the power was out in some parts of the castle and the alarm kept triggering, the screening room had its own generator that seemed unaffected by the B-Force.

A hazy, red light filled the screen. Then words flew out of the haze like comets. They zipped around the screen and came together to form the movie title.

```
THEY !
CAME !
FROM !
PLANET Q !
```

A loud engine revved and a large metal UFO came into view. It was half in the shadows, but I could see it throbbing as if it were *alive* and breathing.

"The first time I watched this with my dad," Jesse whispered to me in the dark, "we spent a week trying to make a miniature replica of the UFO in his laboratory . . ."

"SHHHHHH!" Stella shushed. She's always telling us to be quiet.

Boom-zwah. Boom-zwah.

A low hum-hum noise gave way to a backbeat. It sounded like B-Monster hip-hop—if such a thing existed.

> *They came from Planet Q.*
> *They came 'round here for YOU.*
> *Metal mashing,*
> *Buildings crashing,*
> *City smashing crew!*
> *Robots will land at night.*
> *You think things are all right . . .*

> *But nuts, bolts, screws,*
> *The humans LOSE.*
> *These bots were born to fight.*

All at once, a narrator's voice began to speak . . . real . . . low.

"Once upon a galaxy, there was a mysterious race of robots made of metal and bolts but powered with the soil and rocks of their home planet of Quotidian, known to most as Planet Q," the narrator continued.

All of a sudden two robots appeared on-screen. One of them was holding a rock. Their power stone

was named firequartz and even the tiniest stone contained the magnetism of a thousand conductors and the energy of a thousand fires.

A burst of flames filled the screen. A chorus of violins played in the background, strings screeching. I got goose bumps all over.

"One day, the supply of firequartz grew perilously low. The robots were barely surviving on the dust of the last remaining firequartz stones on their planet. Now they needed to find another source of firequartz—or lose their civilization forever . . .

"Using a special magnetic detector housed in their robot shells, the robots were able to locate the last remaining bed of firequartz rock in the galaxy. They only needed to find one spectacular stone buried deep in the ground of a distant planet . . . a planet called . . .

"EARTH!"

The camera swooped up from the underground into the sky.

"Awesome!" Damon let out a gasp.

Out of a red haze surrounding the opening credits, a huge green and blue orb filled the screen. I could just make out the outline of oceans and continents beneath the massive cloud cover over Earth. Then the camera panned in closer, through the sky and all the way to the ground. It ducked down into a hole in the ground, past worms and roots, until it reached the darkest place ever.

The spooky narrator breathed heavily.

"One rock of firequartz could energize an entire army of Q robots—but how would those robots find it? Could they use their finely sharpened roto-blades to dig deep enough for the stone? The robots formed an armada of spaceships and headed for Earth . . ."

A solitary bot appeared on-screen. It looked exactly like the one in my photo from the mall. Its dark gunmetal body pulsed with red light (fading in and out just like its firequartz energy, of course). The robot rolled out of a smoky red dust and across the ground. It looked fake-o, but what great B-Monster didn't look fake-o? Leery knew what he was doing.

The *They Came from Planet Q* theme music in the background swelled louder and louder and I clutched the armrests of my seat. In the background, a low rumbling thunder sounded like the worst storm ever was brewing.

And then, just as I felt like I wasn't scared anymore . . .

Everything went black.

The screening room was dead silent.

"Is everyone all right?" I said softly.

"You mean even though it's the end of the world as we know it?" Jesse said.

But of course this was just a movie moment. Oswald Leery had us right where he wanted us. A beat later, the rumbling thunder sound effect started up again. There was a bright flash of red. Up on-screen, a faint glow took over the sky. Everything was red. A massive cluster of UFOs circled, headed for the ground, dropped down, and then descended into a wide crater. Dust blew everywhere.

The narrator's voice boomed: "Earthquakes! Panic! Fire! The bots from Planet Q would do whatever they could to get the last remaining firequartz stone in the universe!"

Up on-screen, UFOs transformed into land-roving robots. The bots' metal arms shook in the air. Crooked metal legs covered with loose treads moved across the dusty Earth. The robots probed at stuff with twitching metal antennae that curled out from their heads. Different sized lightbulbs flashed from their midsections, too. Their mouths opened wide, exposing rows of sharp metal. Their robot teeth looked like knives!

The robots moved in and out of the canyon, trying to find the firequartz rock they needed. They moved with great speed at first, but then they started to slow. The journey across space to visit Earth, running on nothing more than firequartz dust, had wiped them out. Soon they would be powerless. But still, they kept up their search.

Each time they dug into a stretch of land, the bots split the Earth and caused tremors and quakes all over. Tremors! That was the shaking we felt inside the mall when we were with Big Wally.

Music played low in the background as the camera slowly pulled back and showed buildings crushed and towers toppling from an aerial view. There were people and cows and even chickens lying by the side of the road. Some had robot tire tracks on their bodies.

"Ewwwwwww!"

My pulse raced hard.

Up on the screen, out of the haze, a man appeared.

Roger Rogers!

In one hand, he carried a camera. My camera, to be exact! He took pictures of all the action around him. In his other hand, he carried something that looked like a gun . . . no, a power drill . . . no, a laser machine . . . no . . .

What *was* that thing?

He aimed it at a break in the firquartz. Then he took aim and fired. There was a blinding white light and then a red, smoky cloud. Before you could say Planet Q, the last remaining firequartz got zapped.

It no longer had any power.

"How cool is that?" Damon whispered to me. "That zapper thing hits the firequartz with so much power and heat that it messes up the magnetic force."

All at once, the movie screen went black. *Again.*

"Is the movie going to come back on in a minute?" I said.

Unfortunately, it wasn't. This was a real-life blackout. The projector's backup generator had finally stopped, too, thanks to all that magnetic interference.

"This happens all the time at the Drive-O-Rama,"

Damon mumbled, trying to sound like he wasn't completely scared out of his wits. "T-t-technical difficulties, that's all."

"Um . . . is anyone else scared?" I asked.

Normally, I don't lose it in the dark, but *this* was no ordinary dark. This was "we're in a spooky castle and there's a monster army of robots coming to get us in about five minutes" dark.

We acted like we were so smart and in control. But it was the B-Monsters who were in control. Outside the castle, at that exact moment, the B-Force was strengthening again. I could only imagine what the mall looked like now!

At that moment, the *real* B-Monster from Planet Q was getting very close, digging, digging, digging . . .

Walter appeared, his face illuminated by a flashlight. He looked like a guy from the haunted house on Halloween.

"I'm so sorry, kids," he said. "Everything's gone kerplooey again! But you already know that."

"What are we supposed to do now?" Stella whispered.

"Is the B-Force getting stronger?" I asked.

"Stronger, yes," Walter said.

"Thanks to the increased magnetism caused by the pending arrival of the movie bots and their retrieval of the firequartz," Jesse said, "I bet the electricity all over Riddle has been short-circuited. That includes this castle."

"Yo, Jess," Damon said. "English, please."

"A changing magnetic field creates electrical current," Jesse said. "So if the magnetism cuts in and out, then the electricity might cut in and out, too . . ."

"Or shutdown completely?" Stella asked.

Walter nodded. "Indeed. Very well said, Jesse."

"Magnets make electricity?" Stella said. "But I thought electrical current created magnetism."

"It works both ways," Jesse explained.

"So the power in the castle is short-circuiting because of all the magnetism?" I asked.

Walter nodded. "Yes, Lindsey," he explained. "When one magnetic force gets hit with another force, like electricity, the molecules inside the object get mixed up . . ."

"And the magnetism goes away!" I said.

Walter nodded. "Exactly. Good work, Lindsey."

"Just a little something I learned from a friend," I said, indicating Jesse, of course.

"Aaaaah!" Damon blurted. His face had gone white. "I can't listen to this science mumbo jumbo anymore. This Monster Squad mission is just too scary for a bunch of fifth-graders. We need Leery. We need an escape route out of Riddle. We need—"

The castle's power rumbled back on and we all looked up. The overhead lights buzzed like wasps again.

Beeeeep! Beeeeep! Beeeeep!

"Aha!" Walter cried, clicking a beeper on his belt. "The communication system is back online! Thank goodness! Let's go get Leery! We have to go before we lose power again! We have a lot to report!"

"And even more to ask," I added.

CHAPTER 8

LEERY THEORY

We raced to the round room near the castle entrance. Leery Castle looked much safer with all the lights turned on. Walter had installed a new, enormous screen monitor for the communicator. We could see Leery almost life-size, speaking to us from halfway across the globe.

When we fought the Beast with 1000 Eyes, Leery had been out of town in the arctic. Today, he was at the Great Wall of China looking for rare specimens of bamboo. I wondered if that meant our next potential B-Monster would be a plant—or distantly related to a panda bear. There was nothing predictable about the Monster Squad. Eventually we'd have to face all B-Monsters: fish, bird, animal, and plant.

Right now the B-Monster was a robot.

The picture on the communicator screen was

crystal clear. We could see Leery as if he were in the room with us. The Great Wall curved for miles in the distance.

"You have come so far since your first Monster Squad mission, my friends," Leery said to all of us.

"Fight the B-Monster! Fight the B-Monster!" Damon yelled out. Stella looked so annoyed. But it didn't bug me. Damon just didn't want to look like a chicken in front of Leery. That was understandable. I wanted to show off every time we came face-to-face with Leery, too.

Walter moved the communicator around so we could each say our own hello. He was in great spirits. He actually greeted me by name.

"Lindsey!" he said. "Walter tells me that you have something that belongs to me . . ."

And then Oswald Leery did something I've never seen him do.

He took off his dark glasses.

It was a little unnerving. After all, his eyes were full of cataracts that turned them a smoky, whitish green color, almost alienlike.

"Hold the camera closer to the screen so I can see it," Leery said in his gravely voice. "I am so pleased that your grandfather saved that camera and that you used it to identify the B-Monster bots. It photographed the B-Force."

"Yeah," Jesse said. "But we still haven't actually seen any bots in the flesh. Well, up close."

Stella pushed me over so she was front and center at the communicator, and not me. I think she was just jealous because Leery talked to me for so long.

And just as Stella stepped up to ask something, Leery's face starting to turn to static. Ha!

Walter hit the control panel and the picture came right back.

"Sometimes I wish I never created *They Came from Planet Q*," Leery said, sighing. "I never should have imagined a world where Earth could be destroyed for good . . ."

"But it can't be! It won't be!" I cried. "We watched the movie again just a few moments ago, Dr. Leery."

"We can get the firequartz away from the robots just like Roger Rogers did," Damon said. "In the movie, Roger Rogers used a contraption he called the 'zapper' to suck all the power out of the firequartz. We can do the same thing!"

"But my friends," Leery said, slipping his glasses on once again. "Roger Rogers was a superhero and you kids are—"

"We're super, too!" Stella cried.

There was silence on the other end of the communicator. Oswald Leery cleared his throat. He faced the camera and smiled.

"You will find the firequartz in the cellar under the mall," Leery said. "I have no record of the coordinates, but it's there. When we made the movie, we mined the entire area and removed most of the stone except for one slab that wouldn't fit in our mine vehicle. But don't be fooled by its size. It might not seem so powerful, but rest assured it is."

As Leery faded from the screen I looked each of my fellow Squadders in the eye. I saw fear, but I also saw resolve. There was only one thing left to do: "Guys, it's time to rock and roll!"

CHAPTER 9

MALL OR NOTHIN'

On the limo ride over to the mall, Jesse started talking science again: magnets, planets, and special forces.

"Tell me again how magnetism works," I said to him.

"The core of Earth is molten iron, which is like this huge magnet. The field of magnetism goes from the north pole to the south pole. And magnetism is the line of—"

"Blah, blah, aaaaah!" Damon groaned. "I see your mouth moving, dude, but I don't get a word of what you're saying."

I chuckled. "He's just trying to help us understand how magnetism works. We need to know these things. We need to know our B-Monster inside and out."

As we got closer to the mall, I kept my eyes glued to the road. We had just passed the Drive-O-Rama drive-in sign and billboard, when Walter hit the brakes—hard.

I whipped out my camera, ready to snap. "What is it? What is it?" I cried.

"Traffic jam!" Walter called back. "Right up there! At the mall entrance. I'm going to have to find another way in."

Walter spun the steering wheel and turned onto a grassy road behind the mall instead.

What a bumpy ride! We were tossed around like popcorn kernels in a pot. One of the limo's car cushions actually flew across the backseat—and I nearly flew across with it! Then a panel in the ceiling clicked open and everything dumped out at our feet: cups, papers, boxes, CDs, rubber bands, envelopes, old magazines. Junk.

"Hey, Lindsey," Jesse said, pointing to one of the papers. "Isn't that a map of the mall?" And sure enough, there on the floor, was a half-crumpled map of the Petroglyph Mall. It must have been left over from when

Leery was devising the bot B-Monsters for *They Came from Planet Q*. What amazing timing! How lucky we were! Even from this distance, way out in the fields, I saw how Petroglyph Mall had grown overrun with people and vehicles and a crazy, swirly storm of objects in the air. The B-Force had gone crazy with blaring sirens and blazing spotlights. The sky was bearing down, too, dark like a storm, like night coming in.

I hated to think what would happen if we didn't figure out how to destroy the B-Monsters before it got pitch-black out here. I could just imagine those red robot lights coming after us in the dark, dark cornfields . . .

Aaaaaaaaaaaaah!

I jumped into the air. Scared myself.

"Look at all those security guards!" Jesse cried. "I bet your dad is over there, Lindsey."

I squinted and I couldn't make out my dad, but I saw at least three times the number of guards stationed there since this morning. We'd only been away from the mall for a matter of hours! In that short time, the B-Force had escalated beyond any of our imaginations! They'd already brought in triple the reinforcements.

Cable news crews were setting up their satellite

dishes, but Jesse said transmissions probably weren't even making it out of the parking lot. The B-Force was growing! Every metal object was becoming magnetized to every other metal object. That's why there had been no reports of this on the news! The news cameras had all stopped working.

As we drove, Walter struggled a little bit with the steering wheel. Something was pulling on the car! Fortunately, Oswald Leery's vehicles come equipped with anti-lock and anti-magnet brakes.

Leery always planned for every emergency.

"Is your skin tingling?" Stella asked. "Because it feels like my skin is tingling . . ."

"Me too," I said.

"We all feel that," Jesse said. "It's the B-Monsters. It's the B-Force. They're almost here."

Indeed, that electric feeling in the air meant the Planet Q robots had to be only seconds away from entering Earth's atmosphere.

I held my breath and counted down to one.

We didn't have a final plan, but we were ready.

5, 4, 3, 2, 1 . . .

CHAPTER 10

MAY THE FORCE
BE WITH US

"My stars!" Walter cried. "The mere presence of the B-Monster has turned the entire mall into an enormous magnetic field! Astounding! If only the crowds knew what was *really* going on. They think it's some kind of strange weather pattern."

This B-Force was as uncontrollable as ever! Every time I went to take a new photograph, the magnetic pull threatened to rip my camera right out of my hands.

We looked over at one of the enormous, overflowing piles of metal objects growing higher than the tallest building in Riddle. Now there was actually a red sports car hanging off it, somehow suspended from a steel girder. In fact, every steel object imaginable, big and small, had made the pile taller and taller. There were horseshoes, hubcaps, power tools, metal fences, a hunk of the divider from the road outside the mall, and a whole bunch of major household appliances.

"This is what must have happened in Spain and in Australia!" I cried. "It's why the metal objects flew out of museums and lawnmowers

shot through the sky! The bots must have flown through all those places . . ."

"Looking for their firequartz!" Jesse said.

"And magnetizing everything big and small!" I added.

The photographers were all around us, scrambling for the best picture and scoop they could get. I knew they couldn't see or photograph the robots (they weren't Monster Squad, after all), but there were plenty of other things to take pictures of. Even the sky made a good photograph right now: It was this deep scarlet red color, like it was on fire.

The magnetism was a problem for some cameramen, who struggled to hang onto cameras while they shot footage of the chaos. More often than not, the magnetism pulled *them* around in addition to their cameras. I saw one guy get lifted all the way up into the air and dropped into the same pile as the washing machines and garbage cans! Luckily, he appeared unhurt.

Walter had smartly bypassed a lot of this magnetic mess by driving as far away from the magnetic pile as he could. He dropped us off in the mall parking lot where no one was parked. While we investigated the B-Monster, he planned to wait with the limo.

We had to hike back to get near the mall, but at least we were safe. I was feeling tougher now. We all were. Stella kept muttering, "Kiiiiiya!" under her breath. We were finally ready for some real action.

"Good luck, Monster Squad," Walter said as we walked away from the limousine. "May the force be . . ."

"With us!" I cheered.

At first we headed directly for chaos central—that is, the mall's front entrance. But then Stella realized that there was no way for us to get inside! Security had every entrance and exit in a major lockdown. I think I saw my dad right there in the middle of it all! If he saw me—or any of us—back here after the evacuation orders, he'd flip a wig.

"I know you don't want to," Stella whispered, "but shouldn't we just ask your dad to let us in?"

"Are you kidding?" I said. "He kicked us out last time—when it wasn't even half as dangerous. There is no way Dad will let us go inside the mall now. Besides, Wally is probably over there, waiting to pounce."

"Who needs Dad?" Damon said. "I have the map from the limousine!"

We all crowded around the map to check it out. There were plenty of entrances marked, but they were all out front.

"Except for here!" Jesse slammed his hand down on the paper. "A loading dock out back. Excellent."

My eyes traced the map from the dock all the way through to a service elevator and downstairs to the mall's lowest level. I wanted to know what obstacles might be in our way. There were a bunch of stores and stalls, but best of all, this map showed fire exits and stairwells. If we were able to slip downstairs, we could bypass some of the main shops and find an entrance to what lay under the mall . . .

Was the mysterious firequartz down there? We hoped so!

The loading dock was located at the far end of Building G. That had to be our way in! The four of us scurried around the mall exterior to the opposite side.

As we walked around, I noticed the sky again. The scarlet red glow had all but turned to black.

"Up in the sky!" Stella cried. "Something is up there!"

"Our B-Monster!" I said. "It's finally here!"

"It's the UFOs from Planet Q!" Damon cried.

They were circling over the mall—dozens of metal B-Monsters—and I did not know what to say or do. The sound was deafening, like a swarm of the creepiest bats ever or a brigade of helicopters with nowhere to land. And the UFOs looked so fake, too, even from far away. It was hard to imagine that this mixed-up mess of bolts could transform into killer, driller robots!

But that's exactly what they were.

"We have to hurry!" Stella said. "We have to find the firequartz rock before they do!"

Stella got to the loading dock entryway first. She tried pressing the control panel for the loading dock door. Then I flipped another switch. Nothing happened.

"Wait! The power is all messed up!" Jesse shouted over the noise around us. "Electromagnetism, remember? It won't let us open the door."

"Look! Over there! A manual lever," Damon said. "Yes!"

We quickly dashed over to a large turning gear. I pulled the gear handle. Stella pulled me. Jesse pulled Stella. Damon pulled Jesse. It only took a few minutes before the door budged. We were able to open it just enough to slip inside.

As I rolled under the door, I glanced up once more at the sky. It was now black with flashes of silver metal. The last of the UFOs were coming in for a landing. Others were already transformed into standing robots with red glowing bulbs on their heads. I blinked hard.

Was this really happening?

"Lindsey! Inside! Quick!" Jesse yelled. Then Damon released the door and it slammed down, narrowly missing my head.

"Now where to?" Damon asked.

I shrugged. I didn't know how to get upstairs from here. We took out the map again and searched for something—anything—that might tell us where to go next. Lucky for us, Jesse had his nifty penlight keychain in his back pocket.

Considering all the crazy noises we'd left outside, this place was a total tomb. The loading dock doors must have been soundproof. And the trouble with scary quiet is that it only makes things that much . . . well, *scarier.* Damon was so jittery, I could barely get him to stop shaking.

Thankfully, we were able to read the map, work our way through the dock's darkness, and find a door marked MALL LOBBY, TWO FLIGHTS UP.

"Everyone ready?" I asked the group. "Because it's mall or nothing from this point on!"

"Ha!" Damon said, cracking a smile.

"All for pun and pun for all!" I joked.

We raised up our four right hands and did a Monster Squad high five . . .

And then we burst through the door like a bunch of TNT.

CHAPTER 11

ATTACK OF THE BOTS

The B-Force inside that part of the building nearly knocked me flat.

The magnetism in the mall was so strong that it lifted me right off my feet for a split second and then deposited me with a swoosh against the window at Burger Stall. It was a good thing that glass didn't break! We grabbed onto poles and nailed down chairs so as not to get carried away. But the force kept pulling me from side to side to . . .

"It's your belt! Undo your belt, Lindsey! It's metal!" Stella shouted.

Quickly, I pulled the belt off and fell to the floor.

Drat that metal belt buckle, I thought.

Everyone else took off

whatever they had on that might be magnetic, too. Stella took off her barrettes and earrings. Damon took off a chain from his neck. Jesse dumped a fistful of coins out of his pocket. I was very glad that my eyeglasses weren't metal. I wouldn't have been able to see a B-Monster without them!

We had to work overtime just to stay on our feet! One false move and we'd find ourselves on some scrap heap in the parking lot. Every second counted.

I pulled out the map again.

Stores with lower level access were marked with symbols, one for each level down.

I wasn't sure I understood a lot of the words and symbols on the map, so I just guessed.

X seemed to be for windows.

Y seemed to be for stairwells.

Z seemed to be for fire lines.

One store had about three different Ys in its space.

"That's the store we need to find!" I cried. It just made sense: The more stairwells the store had, the more access we'd get to the ground floor. "I bet the firequartz is down there somewhere!"

The power was out but the escalators were still accessible. What a difference it made walking here now. No people were in the mall, shoving and pushing us around. We walked the escalator all the way to the lowest level of the mall.

Wow. It was darker than dark down there—and Jesse's penlight didn't do much good.

We'd just reached the very bottom when we heard a boom. Plaster and other building material tumbled down the escalator steps behind us. The quiet of the mall was gone. Had something broken through a wall upstairs?

A Planet Q robot.

Somewhere up above us, in the midst of the rubble, I heard a deep beeping sound. I snapped my camera at the dark and noise.

"LOOK OUT!" Jesse cried.

All at once, we watched as a real, live robot appeared at the top of the escalator. It stood about eight feet tall. And it didn't look happy.

"Oh no!" Damon yelled. We saw a chunk of metal railing at the top. It teetered and tottered.

"IT'S GOING TO FALL!" Stella wailed.

But it didn't fall. It broke off and *flew* up just like the other toys had done that afternoon. It flew up and out of our view. That piece probably went all the way out through the giant hole in the mall ceiling and into one of the many metal piles in the parking lot.

"WHOA!" Damon yelped.

"This is getting scarier!" I cried and Jesse nodded.

We knew that the B-Force was at full force now. The robots had all the power. We had to move fast down here. We turned away from the escalator and followed the map into the belly of the lowest level.

With each step, I snapped more photos. As we

walked past some shops, Jesse and Damon grabbed supplies. They wanted to get a first aid kit and a box of garbage bags. Just in case. We didn't know where we were headed—or how long we'd be down there.

"Stella, where's the store with access doors?" I cried. I needed her to tell me where to run.

But before we could go anywhere, the ceiling above us started to crash in. Another, even bigger robot appeared. It had a bulb glowing on its metal head! It stepped down, narrowly missing us.

Damon freaked out the worst I've ever seen him freak out about *anything*. He actually leaped into Jesse's arms.

Stella the Ninja froze and screamed.

I raised my camera to take a photo, but an incredible thing happened.

My camera started to shake. I wrapped the strap around my wrist and held on for dear life. But it was no use. The magnetic force ripped it right out of my hand.

"Noooooo!" I wailed as the camera went up

into the air, just like all the other objects we'd seen fly today.

But I wasn't about to give up my camera to some B-Monster.

"Give it back!" I wailed. I put up my arms. Stella came alongside me and did the same. Together we yelled out, "KIIIIIIYA!"

All at once, two more huge robots showed up, knocking down a long, white brick wall and crashing through the escalator stairs.

It was like a scene from the movie. I remembered watching the people of Riddle tossed around in a sea of destruction and I didn't want to get tossed around like they had.

"Make a break for it!" I cried.

"We need to find the store with all the *Y*s!" Stella said, waving the map. "It says Store LL310."

I wanted desperately to stay and fight for my camera, but we needed to locate the firequartz. The clock was ticking. The bots were closing in.

Finding anything down here in the half-darkness was impossible. Some storefronts had numbers, some didn't.

Finally we caught up to the right address.

313, 312, 311 . . .

"Here!" Jesse cried.

We stopped in front of the store marked LL310.

"No way," I said with a deep sigh. My whole insides deflated.

I could hardly speak as I read the store's sign: REELY GOOD THINGS.

CHAPTER 12

ARE YOU FOR REEL?!

I could hardly believe it! This was the store where Dad had brought Grandpa Max's camera to be repaired before he gave it to me! I recognized the name right away.

As Damon would say, "Whoa."

Reely Good Things had no people inside, but it had plenty of merchandise, just like Dad said. It was packed to the gills with music players and videos and DVDs galore, including some B-Monster movies. There were shelves of old Oswald Leery movie merchandise, too. Whoever owned this store really was a superfan.

There was even a reel-to-reel machine hooked up to show movies on a back wall. Hence the name: Reely Good. It was the kind of place I would love to explore on any normal day. But this day was anything but normal.

"Quick!" Jesse called out. "Find the access doors. They're supposed to be right here . . ."

"Hey!" Stella said, circling the store. "I don't see anything. They're supposedly right here on the map, but I don't see—"

All at once, Stella leaned against the wall and it began to rotate taking Stella with it. Just like that, she disappeared behind the wall for a moment and then came out the other side.

"Actually, that was fun," Stella giggled.

"Let me try now," Damon said, walking over.

"No!" I shouted. "We don't have time for fun, you guys."

I sounded like Stella.

While we bickered about the doors and how

to find the right stairwell to the basement below, Jesse searched the store shelves for something to help us. He clicked off the reel-to-reel projector and took a look there, too.

Jesse plucked the last reel from the machine and held it up to see the movie.

"Oh, man!" Jesse cried. He looked like he'd just seen a ghost.

"What's wrong?" we asked.

"Read *this* and weep," Jesse said. He held up a reel in his hand. Some of the film unraveled to the floor. The label was half picked off.

THEY CAME FROM PLANET Q

ORIGINAL REEL

"ORIGINAL REEL?" I cried.

"How could this have happened?" Stella asked.

We all raced over and had a look. The reel had been watched—but only halfway.

"Maybe . . ." I said slowly. "If the reel was only half-watched . . ."

"Then only half the movie will come to life?" Stella blurted.

"You guys," I said. "A B-Monster comes alive in the reel's opening segment. After that all bets are off. The rest doesn't matter."

Damon grabbed the reel and shoved it into his backpack. We'd deal with its destruction later. Right now, we had firequartz to find.

"Hey!" Stella called out. She'd wandered to the other side of the store. "Over here!"

Stella pulled back a fancy curtain to reveal another secret door. It was marked on the map as a staircase, but this looked way more like the entry to a bank vault. Stella pushed and pushed but it wouldn't budge.

"It looks as if it has been sealed shut for a century," Jesse said.

"Wait. What's *this*?" Damon shouted. He

rubbed his finger along the edge of the enormous vault-like door. Then he showed us his finger tip. It was covered in a thin coating of red dust.

Red dust!

"Wow," Jesse cried. "Just like Leery said!"

"It's all over my shoes!" I said.

We had to get this heavy door open. The four of us pressed and wiggled, nudged and leaned.

Nothing.

Somewhere upstairs, outside the shop, I heard a loud blast followed by a roar and a crash. More bots had crashed into the mall. They were catching up to us.

"We have to figure this out before the bots destroy the mall!" Stella cried.

"Forget the mall!" I said. "These bots will destroy us!"

"They can't get the firequartz," I said. "Push the door again."

But four fifth-graders—no matter how motivated we were—were still no match for this heavy door.

Damon took off from where we stood.

"Hey!" I cried. "Don't run away again!"

But this time, Damon wasn't running. He was *helping*. Damon Molloy hit a button and the store register's cash drawer went *pa-ping*.

"Hey!" Damon called to us. He held up a key. "What do you think this is for?"

Jesse grabbed the key and dashed over to the vault door. He shoved it right into the lock. Like magic, the key clicked.

As the door opened wide, a swirl of red dust blew into our faces.

CHAPTER 13

THE INCREDIBLE FIREQUARTZ QUEST

"After you," I said to Damon, fanning the dust away from my eyes.

Some of the dust was probably firequartz, but most of the dust was just old cobwebs and floor dirt. This place hadn't been explored in forever. All the dust that had been unearthed during the filming of *They Came from Planet Q* was now whirling through the air like a mini-tornado. It was hard not to cough and sneeze.

"Um . . ." Damon stammered, pinching his nose. "After *you*."

"I knew there was no way that chicken-boy would go step into the untested unknown first!" Stella cried.

"Enough!" I cried. I went in first.

After all of our bad luck *before* entering the mall,

we'd really lucked out finding the reel and the red dust in the same store! We were on a roll.

A *rock and roll*, actually.

Stella and Jesse crowded behind me as we stepped onto the shadowy, stone staircase that (we hoped) led to the firequartz. It was hard to see going down the stairs. Good thing Jesse and Damon had gathered a few supplies, like flashlights—and we still had that penlight.

We went slowly. The red dust left a thick coating on all of the stone steps, which made them slippery.

"No footprints in the dust," Jesse commented. "That means no one else has been here, at least not for a whi—"

CCCCCCCCRASH!

ZZZZZZZZZZZZPPT!

BLOOOOOONK!

"What was *that*?" I stammered. But I knew what it was. And so did everyone else.

The bots were still coming. They sensed the rock. We had to move.

When we got to the bottom of the stairs, Jesse shined the flashlight around.

I couldn't believe the walls. Everything—

everything—seemed to glow red down here. But this was just a room filled with red dust residue—traces of firequartz long gone.

The only source of power in the room was one slab . . . the one Leery had described to us . . .

"Hey, look at Stella!" Damon cried, laughing out loud. Jesse had his light trained on Ninja and she was covered from head to toe in red dust.

"Ugh," Stella said, coughing. Then she pointed at Damon and Jesse and me, too. "Looks like we're *all* covered in firequartz dust, bozo."

We all laughed.

"Wait!" Stella cried. "Do you feel that?"

We all paused.

"Feel what?"

"Air!" Stella said. "I feel fresh, cool air. Where is it coming from?"

Jesse noticed a crack in the wall and the ground. We traced it with the flashlight.

"I bet this crack came from the tremors before the bots got here!" Jesse guessed. "And that's probably when all the red dust swirled around, too! And now that the bots themselves have begun drilling, looking for the last piece of firequartz . . ."

There were jagged cracks in the darker rock. We flashed the light all around to see if the cracks had done more than open a passage for air. Had the cracks created a break in the rocks where we could actually go outside? We might have found an alternate exit from this dark place!

And then, right there, between two of the split slabs, I saw it. It was hardly even noticeable at first, but after a moment or two . . .

The hunk of firequartz rock was right there!

No one knew what to say or do.

"GET IT!" Stella said, assuming her karate pose.

"You get it," Damon grumbled.

We all just stared. It wasn't very big—just like Leery said. It was hard to believe it had much power. But we knew it did. We had to get it out of here . . .

"Grab it and go," Jesse said.

I finally raced over and plucked it out. "We found you!" I cried to the slab of firequartz. It was about the size of a door.

I could have kissed it!

"So now what?" Damon cracked.

"What if . . ." I was thinking on my feet. "We could ask them *nicely* to leave Earth," I offered.

Damon cracked up. "Are you kidding me? Ask them nicely *how*? With flowers and a box of candy?"

"Yeah," Stella laughed. "After we sit down and have lunch together?"

Damon piped up, "And do you speak robot, Lindsey?"

"Um, I hadn't considered the Planet Q language barrier, but—"

"You guys!" Jesse yelled loudly. "I know you're nervous. So am I. But we have to stop talking and start moving. We don't have any more time!"

CCCCCCCCRASH!

ZZZZZZZZZZZPPT!

BLOOOOOONK!

"Oh nooooo!" Stella yelped. "They're all on the level just above us now! They'll be down here soon! What are we going to do?"

"We need a zapper just like Roger Rogers used," Jesse said. "And I have a good idea where we can find one. Grab the firequartz and follow me."

Damon and I took opposite ends of the slab and carried it out. "We can beat these bots," I said with confidence. "Let's go!"

Then Jesse led us through the largest break in the rock wall, out into the loud, hot night.

CHAPTER 14

MAKE IT ZAPPY

When we got upstairs, we could hear the robots all around the mall, breaking up walls and crashing into cars and surrounding the area where we were. The magnetic field was so strong, it practically hummed. I felt it tug at me even though I wasn't carrying or wearing anything metallic anymore.

I imagined the news headline the next day:

Through a set of windows in the mall, I saw a flash of light zapping in the distance. It looked a lot like the sunset earlier that day.

But it wasn't sun. It was lightning. And Damon pointed out the flash wasn't white like normal lighting. It was *red*.

This was B-Monster lightning.

Between the robots and the sunset sky and all this firequartz dust all over my clothes, everything seemed reddish.

I held my breath.

Was the world coming to an end? Had that woman in the mall been right all along?

I had a feeling we'd find our zapper outside. I was counting on Jesse to help pull it together. After all, he was the inventor of the group.

"Hurry!" I cried. "Let's make a break for the front exit. We can get to the big pile faster from there."

"Wait! Stop!" Jesse pointed over toward the mall. We could see the ceiling hole from here. It was bigger than ever and now a large, steely arm poked through. And I was terrified.

More enormous robot arms appeared. Then we saw robot heads. Red bulbs on top glowed like fireballs and they moved a lot more quickly than I expected. Weren't they supposed to be slow and running out of power, after all!?

"Stand here or hide?" Stella asked.

"Hide!" Damon said. He was probably plotting to run away again . . .

"No," I said. "We need to stand up to them. All for one and one for mall!"

From the middle of the bot swarm, one robot appeared that was even bigger than the rest. It had three bulbs on its head!

"Oh no! Who is *that*?" Jesse asked.

Damon looked at him funny. "I thought you knew everything, dude."

The supersized robot leaped toward us. All around it were the red laser beams, flashing like a portable electrical storm. But it looked a little sluggish. One thing was for sure: That bot had its eyes on me like I was dinner.

All at once, as the leader bot approached, my head tingled and my hair started to stand up on end. I noticed Damon's and Jesse's hair, and Stella's, too. With a last-minute surge of power, our hair went vertical—electrified!

The moment to act was NOW.

Without thinking, I snatched the slab out of Damon's hand and rushed out in front of that giant bot all by myself. I don't know where I got the strength to carry that slab on my own. You know that story about a grandma who lifted a car to get to her kitty-cat out from underneath? I felt like that grandma.

Raaaaaaaaaaaaaaaarrgh!

As I rushed forward, the biggest robot paused and raised up his steely arm. I held up that very large chunk of firequartz in front of me, sort of like an offering. I was testing the bot.

Would he take it?

"Stop!" Stella screamed. "He's going to squash us like pancakes, I just know it. Lindsey, back up! Run away! This is dangerous!"

"No, he sees the rock!" Damon cried. "Way to go, Lindsey! He sees the rock! He wants the rock!"

He wants the rock!

Turns out, he didn't go for the rock.

Instead he grabbed *me* and lifted me high into the air. I lost my grip and the slab went careening for the ground, breaking it in two.

MAGNETIC NO MORE

I screamed.

Well, of course I screamed.

Who wouldn't scream if a massive robot from outer space grabbed her with its metal claw?

"Lindsey!" the other three members of the Monster Squad cried. They were screaming, too—a lot. From where I was dangling, I could see them waving their arms around, too.

Damon turned white as a ghost. No big surprise there.

Stella had assumed her usual "I'm gonna kick your butt" pose. Hard to believe that she actually thought she could take on thirty-six robots! But she was always ready to try!

I could not see Jesse, though. Had the robots gotten him, too?

I swooshed through the air. The giant robot was not wasting any more time. He didn't care about bargains or deals. *He wanted me.*

I was a goner.

"Hey!" I yelled. "Tell my mom and dad I love them, will ya?"

The noise in the parking lot outside the mall was deafening. With all of our focus on getting the bots, I'd forgotten just how noisy and nuts the mall had become. From up here, I could see everything spread out for an acre or more. I wondered if Walter could see me, up here, clenched by this B-Monster. This was *so* not how I wanted to end today.

All of a sudden, without warning, the robot opened its claw and let me roll right out.

Thunk.

I landed hard on the ground.

I was alive! I was free! I was . . . *confused.*

I darted back over to Stella and Damon, gasping for air.

"What happened?" I said. "Why did it let go of me?"

"Look at yourself," Stella said. "The bot thought *you* were the firequartz rock. You're covered in red dust. It got mixed-up."

"Where's Jesse?" I asked. "Where's the rock?"

Jesse let out a whoop and a howl. "I'm over here!" he cried. "FIREQUARTZ IS OVER HERE!"

He wanted us—and the robots—to hear him.

What a fabulous photo opportunity that scene would have made! We watched as the army of bots turned their attention—and their clunky bodies—toward Jesse. Now they were definitely moving more slowly.

Damon and Jesse each took a slab of the split firequartz and raised it over their heads. The bots moved toward them.

What were we supposed to do?

"Follow me!" Jesse bellowed.

Their eyes were on the stone.

"To the left," Jesse called out to Damon. They moved from side to side like they were on the TV show *Stars Who Dance*.

When Jesse and Damon ran to the left, the Bots ran to the left. Then Jesse signaled to Damon to switch to the right. They switched and ran right . . . and left . . . and right. They zigzagged in circles, lugging the heavy rock close to their chests. The bots tried to keep up.

But they couldn't.

Some stumbled and tripped over their own robot feet. Others slowed to a stop. The robot leader was the only one who was keeping up—and even its red bulbs were beginning to dim.

Jesse and Damon were winning! Monster Squad was winning!

Stella and I ran to catch up with the boys.

"What are you doing?" I cried to Jesse. "You're a genius!"

"Hurry up!" Jesse said. "I have a master plan. We have to get the firequartz over there!"

Jesse pointed to another part of the parking lot where tons of power lines had gone down. One cable whipped in the air, blue sparks crackling.

A zapper!

"If we could just aim that cable at the rock, we could use it to destroy the rock."

"Why can't we?" I asked.

"Because it's pretty unsafe," said Jesse.

"You know what else is unsafe?" Stella asked. She paused three beats for effect. "Robots who want to destroy humankind."

CHAPTER 16

PHOTO FINISH

We decided to risk it. Or, to be exact, we decided *I'd* risk it. Luckily we were standing next to the mall that just threw up. There were clothes all over the place. So I made myself a protective suit out of rubber gloves, a scuba mask, and a man's down jacket that went all the way to my ankles. It wasn't much of a fashion statement, but I figured it would do the trick.

"Okay, Lindsey," Jesse coached. "Just aim that cable toward the rock and let the sparks do their thing. The last firequartz will be destroyed just like in the movie. It'll be like Walter said. All the molecules will get confused. And the bots will be magnetic no more."

I took a deep breath. Then I grabbed the end of the cable and aimed it toward the rock. "Don't try

I was searching the piles of metal objects for one important prop from *They Came from Planet Q.* Let me tell you, my pile-climbing days are *way* behind me. Phew!"

The dial on top of the camera was broken, but I didn't care. I was just happy to have it back.

Walter turned the key in the ignition and we started to drive away, but Damon screamed from the backseat.

"WAIT! STOP!"

The limo came to a screeching halt.

Oh no, I thought to myself. *What could possibly be the matter now?*

Damon reached into his backpack and pulled out the original reel of *They Came from Planet Q.*

"We forgot to destroy the movie!" he cried. "Can you imagine if, after all that, we never even got rid of the reel? We have to do this—now."

"Yes, we do," Walter said.

I grabbed the reel out of Damon's hands. "Here, let me do it," I said.

In a way, this had been my battle all along. I hopped out of the car and dropped the reel in front of the limo tires.

"Okay, drive!" I commanded.

Walter knew exactly what to do. He drove back and forth and forth and back over the reel, until it was smooshed to smithereens. After that, I picked apart whatever wasn't destroyed by the wheels of the car, piece by piece. In no time, the original reel was nothing more than a bunch of shreds.

I got back into the limousine with my broken camera and one of those shreds (just for a random souvenir).

"Uh . . . can we go home now?" Damon asked.

We all laughed. I was sad about the camera, but home sounded so good. I was glad we were driving with Walter, too. We got home extra fast.

Once inside my house, I raced past Mom so she wouldn't see me covered in red dust from the mall. I changed out of my clothes and took a shower before heading back downstairs with the broken camera. I wanted to put it away safely in my darkroom.

"Have fun with your friends?" Mom asked when I came back down.

I nodded. "Yup."

"No more bugging your father at work, I presume?" Mom asked.

"Uh . . . nope."

She has no idea that we just destroyed an entire alien robot army! I thought. *Incredible!*

"Okay," Mom said, just like every other night. "Dinner will be ready soon. Your dad called. Apparently there's been some major hubbub at the mall all day. Good thing you went this morning, dear, or else you might have gotten mixed up in it!"

"Yeah," I said. "That would have been a bad thing."

I turned and sneaked down to the basement with my broken camera.

The darkroom down there seemed empty with just me developing stuff in there. It had been so much fun to have my fellow Monster Squad members here, developing photos together and planning our counterattack on the bots.

So much had happened in one day.

I flopped on the sofa and looked hard at the camera. The dial was completely busted. I contemplated fixing it with super-duper glue, but no matter how hard I tried, I wouldn't get it to work like before. It needed B-Force. It needed those bots. It needed red lightning.

Even broken, however, the camera could still be the star of my collection. So I placed it up on the shelf.

"LINDSEY!" Mom called out from upstairs. "*Word Buzz* is on! Want to play?"

"I'm tired, Mom," I said. "Not tonight."

"Tired?" Mom cried. "What could possibly have tired you out so much?"

I sank back into the downstairs couch and just closed my eyes. There were so many things to "B" tired about. Ha-ha. Someday, I'd tell Mom about all of them—and about all of our great Monster Squad adventures. I'd even show her the photos.

But for now, I just wanted to catch up on some sleep so I'd be rested up in time for the next Monster Squad mission. Somewhere out there, the next B-Force was already brewing.

this at home," I shouted, wagging my finger at my fellow Squadders. My heart was practically pounding through the down jacket as I carefully picked up the cable, held it as far from my body as I could, and aimed it directly at the firequartz.

There was a blinding white light and then a red, smoky cloud. Those bots didn't know what hit 'em. Or rather, what zapped 'em. One by one, starting with the biggest bot, the Planet Q creatures began to fall to pieces until they were reduced to a pile of big, old, busted bots—literally.

We jumped into the air, shrieking. Not that anyone could hear us. The sirens around us were still sounding. The mall was still a great big mess.

But the disaster wasn't over yet.

All at once, even over all that noise, we heard a loud screech. We turned our heads in time to see each of the enormous magnetized piles in the parking lot . . . come undone.

One car on the top of the car pile bumped its way over the side; a few washing machines and a plow shovel went next. Coins were flying off another pile, as were other metal objects of all sizes. The noise was incredible. People ran screaming. Without the bots or the firequartz to throw off Earth's magnetic field, everything that had been magnetized came undone. It was a metallic landslide.

How would the scientists explain this one? I wondered. It felt pretty cool to know that Monster

Squad knew more than most people about the events that had just taken place. Leery was right. Being in the squad was an *awesome* responsibility.

Just then, Walter pulled up in the limousine.

"I don't believe it!" Walter cried, racing from the front seat to meet us. "You beat the bots! Dr. Leery will be so proud! Jesse, the power line zapper was a stroke of genius. Lindsey, your bravery was next to none. Bravo, Monster Squad! Now hop in and let's get away from this disaster!"

Jesse, Stella, Damon, and I piled into the limousine.

It was hard to calm down after the excitement of the bot battle. Everyone was positively giddy with happiness over our victory.

But a little part of me felt sad.

"Why so glum, chum?" Walter asked, eyeing me in the rearview mirror just like he always did.

"My camera," I said. "Grandpa Max's camera. The giant robot took it and now it's lost forever."

"Ahh," Walter said. "I see."

Then he lifted something off the front seat and held it up for me.

It was my camera! I grabbed it and kissed it. "Thank you! Thank you!" I said. "But how did you get it?!"

"Oswald Leery wasn't about to lose this again," Walter said. "While you kids were fighting the bots,